LB kids is an imprint of
Little, Brown and Company Books for Young Readers.
The logo design and name, LB kids, are trademarks.

Visit our website at www.lb-kids.com

ISBN 0-316-01776-0

First Edition: October 2006
Manufactured in Malaysia.

10 9 8 7 6 5 4 3 2 1

Janet and Allan Ahlberg

THE JOLLY POSTMAN
or *Other People's Letters*

LITTLE, BROWN & COMPANY

LB kids™

NEW YORK BOSTON LONDON

Once upon a bicycle,
   So they say,
A Jolly Postman came one day
   From over the hills
And far away . . .

With a letter for the Three Bears.

Mr and Mrs Bear
Three Bears Cottage
The Woods

So the Bears read the letter (except Baby Bear),
    The Postman drank his tea,
And what happened next
    We'll very soon see.

Off went the Postman,
    Toodle-oo!
In his uniform of postal blue
    To a gingerbread cottage –
And garage too!

With a letter for the Wicked Witch.

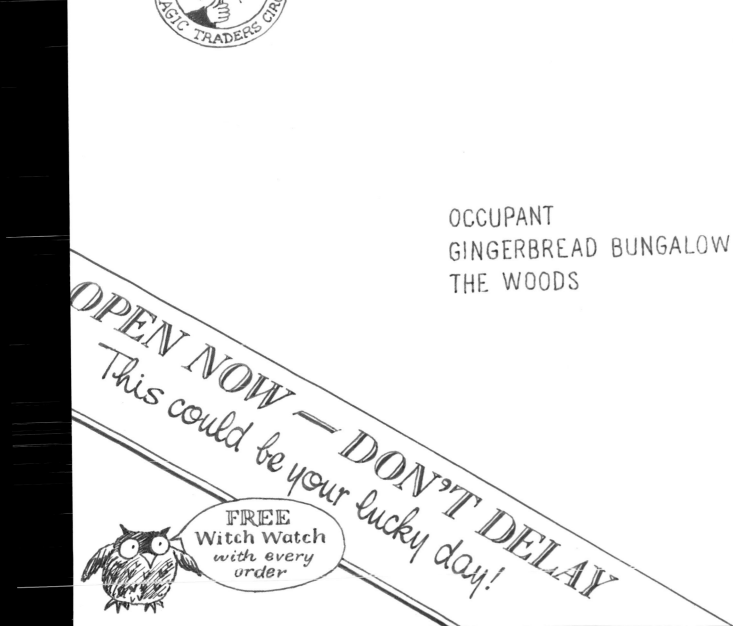

If undelivered return to...

HOBGOBLIN SUPPLIES LTD.
WARLOCK MOUNTAIN
DEPT. 46A.

So the Witch read the letter
With a cackle of glee
While the Postman read the paper
But *left* his tea. (It was green!)

Soon the Jolly Postman,
  We hear tell,
Stopped at a door with a giant bell
  And a giant
Bottle of milk as well,

With a *postcard* for . . . guess who?

PAR AVION
VIA AIR MAIL

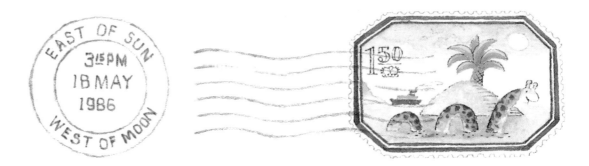

EAST OF SUN
3¹⁵PM
18 MAY
1986
WEST OF MOON

1⁵⁰

MR. V. BIGG
MILE-HIGH HOUSE
BEANSTALK GARDENS

So the Giant read the postcard
With Baby on his knee,
And the Postman wet his whistle
With a thimbleful of tea.

Once more on his bicycle
    The Postman rode
To a beautiful palace, so we've been told,
    Where nightingales sang
And a sign said SOLD,

With a letter for . . . Cinderella.
(There's a surprise!)

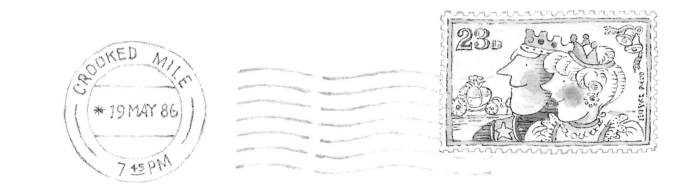

H. R. H. Cinderella

The Palace

Half Kingdom Road

So Cinders read her little book,
    The Postman drank champagne
Then wobbled off
    On his round again
        (and again and again – Oops!)

Later on, the Postman,
   Feeling hot,
Came upon a "grandma" in a shady spot;
   But "Grandma" –
What big *teeth* you've got!

Besides, this is a letter for . . . Oooh!

URGENT

B. B. Wolf Esq.
C/o Grandma's Cottage
Horner's Corner

So "Grandma" read the letter
  And poured the tea,
Which the not-so-Jolly Postman
  Drank . . . nervously.

Now the Jolly Postman,
    Nearly done (so is the story),
Came to a house where a party had begun.
    On the step
Was a Bear with a bun.

But the letter was for . . . Goldilocks.

PLEASE DO NOT BEND

FAR AWAY
20. V. 86.
S. W.

To

Goldilocks

24 Blackbird Road

Banbury Cross

So Goldilocks put the money
    In the pocket of her dress,
Asked the Postman to her party
    And, of course, he answered, "Yes!"

Once upon a bicycle,
  So they say,
A Jolly Postman came one day
  From over the hills
And far away . . .

And went home in the evening – for tea!

The End